WISE WIVES BUILD
REDEMPTION

CASSANDRA L. WILLIAMS

Wise Wives Build Redemption

Copyright © 2019 Cassandra Williams

ISBN-13: 978-0-578-57569-8

ISBN-10: 0-578-57569-8

Books can be ordered online or by contacting:

Cassandra Williams Enterprises

130 Prominence Point Pkwy

Suite 130-209

Canton, GA 30114

(404) 259-2690

Website: www.thecassanndrawilliams.com

Email: info@thecassandrarwilliams.com

This book is dedicated to every person that has found themselves drowning in the sea of guilt and shame at the brink of despair. May hope and comfort guide you home… to the original purpose for your life. What you have done is not who you are.

"We could all use a little redemption." — *Amy Wolf*

TABLE OF CONTENTS

INTRODUCTION

So here I was standing at the door to an amazing life looking like a million bucks. Much of my furniture and the myriad of boxes filled with clothing, jewelry, makeup, kitchen items and more were all inside. Unbeknownst to my new husband, I had so much more that I was carrying. It was invisible to the naked eye, but I felt the weight daily. This baggage wasn't created in a factory by Gucci or Prada but years and years of disappointment, heartache, and *love* (or lack of it) from those I thought would protect and care for me.

I had no words to explain what went on daily in my mind and what kept me from loving at one hundred percent. You know that unconditional love that allows you to trust. Yeah…that part. There were compartments and doors that had been locked with the keys thrown away years ago. The wedding day was perfect from the hair, dress, makeup, and food to the A1 guest list. It had been 3 years in the making. Now, all that was left was to take that step over the threshold into this new life. I was somebody's wife. Me. The girl that had vowed never to marry but focus on work and becoming a billionaire. The girl that never thought a guy could look at her without being disgusted. Me, the girl that loved hard and was always let down harder. Sure, I knew how to cook, clean, provide sexual pleasure, and be the pretty trophy in his arm, but…

I didn't know how to hold my tongue and let cooler heads prevail.

I didn't know that my tone was sharp enough to cut through his soul like butter.

I didn't know how to support him when I didn't understand or agree.

I didn't know what it truly meant for him to be the head and me to be his helpmate.

I didn't know that men battle insecurity and fear as much as women do.

There was so much I didn't know, but I was about to learn. This is my journey to pulling down the intricate framework formed in the mind of a little girl and becoming a wise wife that knows how to build up her home instead of tearing it down.

CHAPTER 1

My name is Amira Joy, AJ for short. I grew up in a time where children were seen and not heard. Anytime you found yourself in a room with people speaking about topics that were inappropriate for young ears, I would hear the statement, "Grown folks talking." No other direction needed to be given. I knew to get up and go to my room or outside to play. I could be anywhere but where they were talking.

Seven-year old me once asked Michelle, the neighbor's daughter what she thought her mom and mine were talking about after they kicked us out of the living room so they could talk.

"They are talking about something bad," Michelle said. She was eight.

I looked at her curiously. I wasn't sure of that.

"When grown people talk, they talk about bad things. Like weed or cigarette, or like crime or their husbands."

I had no clue what she was talking about. She looked like she had no clue as well.

"It's what my uncle told me," she added.

"What are they talking about now?" I asked.

"I don't know. Maybe they want to kill someone."

Such naivety! That little discussion with Michelle piqued my interest. I'd find myself eavesdropping from time to time, only hearing bits and pieces of the conversation and allowing my mind to fill in the rest and draw up its own conclusions. Quite easily, I'd say. Those early years had a lot of impact on the person I became.

Coming from a small town in Georgia, we lived on the other side of the tracks. There was mom, who was the queen of the dismissive 'grown folks talking', and grandma whose mantra was, 'sin will do you no good'. There, everyone knew everyone, and you were constantly privy to the lives and issues they had. Grandma's house was a rallying center. She ran a daycare, and there was always a spare bed for anyone who needed it.

Life choices and lifestyle were things I observed and learned from daily. I once asked my grandma why a grown man was sitting and weeping in the living room. "He's homeless," she told me. "His wife caught him cheating and filed for divorce."

"Does divorce make people cry?" I asked.

"Well, if you're going to become homeless afterwards, it might."

"I don't get it, grandma."

"The house belongs to his wife. She bought it before they got married a year ago."

The wheels of my little mind were turning.

Marriage and the issues that came with it were things I learned about from books, movies, TV shows and general observation. I watched grownups interact and took note of what to do or not to do; what I was willing to take and not willing to take. The Dos and Don'ts seemed simple enough. Why the heck did people still fail at it?

The framework with which to process situations I'd encounter in marriage was being built. Television shows and movies were also deceptive. If you got mad or it wasn't working out, you just left. Of course, it had to be in a blaze of glory with lots of yelling and slamming of doors. Marriage was a contract not a covenant, they'd purport. There was little to no respect for the vows that were taken. Well, I guess they really didn't take them. It was all make believe... a script.

How do you agree to be with someone for the rest of your life and in less than a year, you prefer sex with others?

Then there were the lies people fabricated and wallowed in. Their homes were chaotic, but outside they'd smile like there were a million cameras outside the door as they stepped out. They even took their hypocrisy to church. Church folks would hug and smile with you but walked right pass you in the grocery store; the friendly deacon would forget how to wave once he was with his wife.

An incident happened at home that further formed my psyche of people. Patricia lived with us for about five months. She preferred it when we called her Miss Tricia. She was beautiful and soft spoken. One day, she packed her things and left. I couldn't understand it.

"But why would she leave like that?" I asked grandma when I found her tending to her flowers.

"It is not her fault," she said to me. She looked unperturbed.

"It was yours then? Did you send her away?"

"You know I don't send people away. When I said it was not her fault, I meant she doesn't know how else to live. Did you know she was married? She loved her husband. They had a small store in town. It wasn't making good money, but it was enough to keep them fed. They were building together. At least they believed that. She took ill and was in the hospital. During that time, her husband sold the store and left town with another woman. She was broken. She came to live here. I don't think my help was enough. She had already learned how to abandon people—just the way she was abandoned."

"It is sad." I remember feeling bad about the situation. I liked Miss Tricia.

I saw these things so much it left me with a marred view of people. By the time Bellamy showed up, I had a list of items that were nonnegotiable. I am not going to do this; he better not do that. If he does this, then I am going to do that. He better come with this figure in his bank account. Well, guess what? He had a list, too. Now here we were starting a life together with two lists that had not been communicated. I had concerns he expected me to do what his mom did. I expected him to do what my dad did or didn't do. We'll talk more about that later. The impact of what I saw reached farther and deeper in my marriage than most of what I heard.

CHAPTER 2

L ike other little girls, I would sit by the window and eagerly await my dad's arrival from work. It was frustrating for me when he delayed. I'd be restless and bother mom so much she'd pick up the phone and dial his office number. Then she'd tell me he was on his way back. When dad came in, I'd be in his arm until she made him put me down so he could change into his house clothes.

He didn't speak a lot. In fact, he wasn't the type of dad that told nighttime stories. His presence usually was enough for me. When his presence didn't do it, the ice cream he bought sure did. I loved when he took me out for ice cream and pizza and would buy enough to leave me gorged. Back home, we would watch TV until we both fell asleep on the couch. We ignored mom's bedtime rule for me. He was an easy-going man.

One day he left home and never came back. He died. He worked as a construction worker. His hands were hard from the work he did, his heart a reeling contrast. Touching his hands, I used to be fascinated by how strong he was. It seemed his heart wasn't as strong; it gave up on that day. Heart attack. He left me with a hole in the heart.

I couldn't grasp the effect growing up without a father would have on me. I was eight when he died. I missed his presence, but that was the easy part. A ripple I was oblivious of was already spanning into my adult life.

We went to live with grandma. On the bus ride there, I asked mom; "We will see him again, right? Dad, we will see him, right?"

"Darling, we won't," she said, shaking her head. "Dying is not a temporary thing, it is permanent."

I couldn't accept that. It didn't make sense. Mom tried to help. "You will be fine. We will be fine."

"No, we won't."

She took a deep breath. "You see how you lost a tooth, and you had to cry. I told you you'll be fine. Now look how fine you are, another tooth grew to replace it. We are going to grandma's house; she will take care of us."

Mom shouldn't have made that analogy, because whenever I went in front of the bathroom mirror to brush, my teeth reminded me of my missing dad, and there was still nothing to replace him.

A father provides identity even from the womb. No, this is not a physical science lesson but just the truth. A father is a young girl's first example of how a man is supposed to treat a woman. If he treats her like a princess and validates her, she is less likely to fall for the foolishness that some boys try. She won't look for validation and acceptance because she has already been accepted by her father. His presence matters even when his words are few. That was taken away from me the afternoon he died.

There was no one to protect me. There were no father daughter dances. He didn't show up for career day so I could show him off to all the other kids. He didn't get to teach me how to drive or walk me down the aisle and hand me over to Bellamy. I knew how to cope when they leave, but I didn't really know what it meant for a good man to stay and provide for the family. Remember I depended on friends, family and the television for all my relationship advice.

Yes. I know my dad would have stayed with me if he could but that did not stop the feelings of anger, rejection and abandonment. I searched for someone or something to fill the void, to fulfil the longing I felt deep inside. I often ignored the red flags that directed me to run for the hills because of boredom. Relationships were just something to pass the time. I attracted many con men because they saw my brokenness and wanted to exploit it. They said all the right things in all the right moments, and I found myself falling. Falling in and out of love, despair, and insecurity. I was a beautiful mess with a temper to match. No one understood my pain. Everyone thought I was too young to remember him or be adversely affected by his absence. They were wrong, all of them.

Apparently, it wasn't only me who missed him. I found mom several times in the room sobbing. She tried her best to hide why she cried, but I knew. She hadn't found it possible to replace him as well.

Bellamy came into my life like a cool breeze on a hot summer's day. We met through a mutual friend. We were both being introduced to other people. Ironically, they didn't show up. I didn't really think much was going to happen that day. I thought love was overrated. I was driven and a lasting relationship was not on my radar, but we hit it off. It wasn't particularly down to his persistence or my curiosity (I had stopped being a curious girl by then), it just happened. Dates and dates and a few more, and a relationship had landed on my lap.

On one of the dinner dates, he asked me; "How did you grow up?"

I thought about it for a while, and I didn't know how to answer. People usually asked, *where did you grow up?* and half the time, they aren't paying attention to your response. I realized then he wanted to know me... my story.

"I don't know where to begin," I said to him.

"From the beginning... from the point you can remember," he said.

"That's a lot."

"I'm not working tomorrow. Unless you are, then we're good."

It was Friday night, of course I wasn't going to work the next day. The truth is, one would really be foolish to bother people with their life story if they were only going to see each other for a couple of times.

Sensing my reluctance, he said; "I will tell you about me. I grew up in North Carolina. Life was fine, good parenting, mom and dad were present as much as they could. They worked, you know that's usually the way average people pull through in these times. Both parents have got to work. I was bright as a kid, stupid as a teenager. Got my..."

"Stupid?" I asked.

"Yes, stupid," he said.

He told me more about that. He had landed himself in some trouble in his earlier years. A mistake he still regretted, and had done everything in his power to never repeat. He had since moved on, and had materials reflecting this time of his life in his songs. Yes, as part of the things he did, he was a recording artist.

His openness broke the layers of ice for me. I told him about myself. I never knew how much I had to share until I started talking. Perhaps it was the fact that I had someone so willing to listen, so calm and encouraging that I couldn't' stop talking. I went deep without knowing it. I found myself in tears. I had been talking about how much I would have loved my father to have stayed. I didn't know I'd find myself in that state.

Bellamy understood and knew how to show it. I knew he was different because he listened, and he didn't act like all the other guys. He was gentle and patient with me much like the character of God. Every time we went out, he wanted to know my inner thoughts. He wanted my opinion. He was willing to understand me. I didn't feel like I was a rest-stop on his way to his real destination. He hit many brick walls, but the consistency in his character paid off.

I often wondered how all the other women in his life missed such a jewel – a diamond neglected. I started out praying that I could be the woman he wanted me to be. That later shifted to, 'Lord make me the woman you created me to be so I can minister to him the way he needs'.

The first time I was at Bellamy's, I didn't know the best way to act. It was the first time I found myself contemplating my actions and my words around a man.

"I hope the apartment isn't too humble for you," he said to me.

I smiled. His home was modest. He was as free as he wanted. He opened a bottle of champagne and poured two glasses. He let his glass sit. It was easy to see he wasn't much of a drinker. For me, I didn't know how much was enough.

After some time, he took a look at me and smiled. "You're famished, darling, I can tell."

I was. I was taken aback that he found that so obvious.

"The closest I can get to food is Chinese," he said. "I'll place an order right away if that's fine with you."

"Ummm, I think I'll pass on Chinese. It's not really my thing.

"Oh. Well then, the closest option except that might take as much as forty minutes to arrive. You know what, I'll just fix you something in the kitchen." He got up and said, "Give me a little time."

I was pleased. Then I became troubled. Perhaps it would be better if I joined him in the kitchen, I thought. I wanted to be right for him. I felt he was right for me. In the weeks to come, I found myself trying to do things to please him.

As long as I was trying to be what he wanted, I was being someone I wasn't created to be and trying to be perfect. Perfection was another box that I tried to reside in that led to many sleepless nights and disappointments. That need to be perfect and to maintain an image in front of people was a stronghold that had to be broken for me to be authentically me. This need to be wanted or needed would lead me to try and fill the void with all the wrong things and people.

A few months after our relationship started, I traveled to visit my mom. She still lived in my grandma's house, even though she had now passed on. We sat at the veranda while she asked about work and how I was doing.

"You haven't been home since your last promotion," she said to me, sipping from her cup of hot herbal tea. "How are you managing the stress?"

"There's no stress, mom," I said, shrugging.

"Don't lie to me, girl. The vice president of the company, and, and… didn't you tell me you close million dollar deals daily? That's got to be packed with stress."

"Not necessarily. But I understand your concerns. I got trained for this. I'm used to it. And I'm handling it well."

She looked at me for a while. "Miss Modest. The Lord is your strength." I smiled. "Do you still pray?" she asked.

"Of course, mom."

"Alright. Do you still go to church?"

"I do."

She sipped more tea and was silent for a while. Then she turned to me again. "Are you seeing someone now?"

I was waiting for that. so typical of her to ask. Before I could answer, she said; "Don't tell me you're still into that non-sense."

"What nonsense?" I asked. I knew exactly what she meant. She had heard me repeatedly swear I didn't care about relation-ship, and that I was into the money-ship.

"You know what I'm saying," she said.

I took a deep breath. "I'm seeing someone." The smile on her face was priceless. It didn't last long. It was replaced with skepticism. "I mean it."

"Alright. Who is he?"

"You mean, she?" The warmth left her face. I laughed. "Just kidding, mom," I said and kissed her on the cheek. "His name is Bellamy."

She looked at me. Convinced I meant it, she asked; "Is he a good man?"

I nodded pleasantly. "Very good. He is a very good man."

She looked at me until beads of tears formed in her eyes. She tried to blink it away. "Your face, your cheeks, they are round and shinning. I haven't seen them like this in a long time."

"Really?"

"That's how your cheeks are when you are pleasantly happy. I remember when your dad would come home from work, and you'd run into his arm. Your cheeks were usually like this—round and shinning."

I didn't know what to say. Without warning, I was hauled into memory lane. The images were faintly. They were images of my dad standing by the doorway asking—*where is my princess?*

"I remember how you'd be restless, waiting for him," mom said. "You'd make me dial his office number so I could ask him to come home to you." She sighed. "I never really dialed his office line. I pretended to. But it always made you feel better whenever I did."

That night, I cried like I hadn't in a long time. My body shook as I thought of how my life might have been had dad been around longer.

CHAPTER 3

"Grandma, who is this?" I asked, standing and looking up at the portrait of a lady in white on the wall. I had seen that photo in her room for more than two years I lived there but never bothered to ask.

"Oh, that would be my mother, your great grandmother."

"She was quite beautiful."

"That she was. Never looked anything like what she went through."

"She went through a lot?"

"Oh she did. You know she's the inspiration behind the daycare I run."

"How's that?"

Grandma came and stood by my side, looking up at the portrait as I did. "She got cheated out on a deal because she didn't understand what was stated in the contracts. She learned the hard way; ignorance was no excuse. So she had the mind to help with education for whoever wanted it. She made sure I was schooled. I made sure your mother was as well. When I set up the daycare and the basic learning class, she was overjoyed. She was alive then. She said it was one of her best days on earth."

"She must have been a good woman."

Grandma simply nodded slowly. It was easy to see she was reminiscing. "So good," she said finally. "Strong as well. She was a pillar."

I heard the stories of my great grandmother, but I watched the strength and resilience that my grandmother, my mother and my aunts exhibited. I was taught I could be anything I wanted to be. *Can't* was not a word that I could use. Adversity was met with *try harder* or *find another way*, legally of course. What didn't kill you only made you stronger. I used to laugh when I heard them say that, as I got older, I understood the power in those words.

I watched the women in my family take care of their families with grace and poise. There was always a hot meal and a warm place to lay your head. That comfort was extended to those outside the scope of immediate family. The only reason you lived on the street or lacked a meal was because you chose it. As I said before, women were supposed to cook, clean, and take care of the family, right? There were times I wondered if my mom and grandmother wanted more.

I didn't understand being home for your family as a necessity. I was concerned with money. I knew they could make more money working outside the home, but I didn't realize what they would be giving up by missing sporting events and school assemblies. I naively saw their sacrifices as a weakness or something undesirable. I made a vow that that would not be my story.

I was at the grocery store with mom one evening when a woman, obviously not familiar with the stores layout, asked her; "Please ma'am, any idea where they keep the fresh veggies?"

Mom pointed her in the right direction with a smile. I watched the woman go. She was dressed in a classy, yet formal way. I was fascinated by her.

"Mom, that woman… she looks successful."

Mom looked at her receding frame. "Maybe," she said.

"Why aren't you successful like that?"

Mom looked at me, her thirteen-year-old curious daughter, for some time before moving on along the aisle. I wondered if I had offended her. On our way home, she turned to me.

"You see, Amira, success is subjective. You set a goal, and you try to achieve it. When you do, that's success. No goal particularly outshines the other. I take a look at you and I see a flourishing young girl, nurtured and happy, that's success for me. If it were any other way, then I'd see myself as a failure."

"You're saying I am your success?"

"Yes, a part of it. A big part of it. I wouldn't think I was successful if I didn't know where to pick the best vegetables to make a nice meal for my family."

It took a long time for me to wrap my head around that one. Although I saw the women in my life perform miracles with two fish and five loaves of bread, I wanted the life of luxury and everything that came along with it. Silly to think about all that now. As I look around at my life, I am rich in more ways than money.

We returned home that day to find Grandma enraged. I had never seen her that way before. When she saw me come into the living room, she ordered me to leave for my room. "Grownups got to talk," she said.

Later, I went into her room to talk to her. "Grandma?" She looked up at me from her sewing machine. "You were mad at me," I said. "I'm sorry if I did something wrong."

I loved grandma so much. I preferred days when my mom was mad at me. Grandma was just so sweet it took a lot to piss her off.

"Oh darling, I was not. Come…" I walked over to her and she cuddled me. "I was not mad at you. I'm sorry for sounding mean to you."

I was pleased she was not mad with me, and even more curious with why she was mad. "Is something wrong, grandma?" I asked. "You looked pretty angry earlier."

"No, darling, nothing is wrong. Well, it was, but it's fine now."

"Okay." I began to leave the room.

"Oh, come back here," she said. "This may be a teachable moment for you." She made me sit before she started talking. "Before you and your mom came to live here, there was this young girl who lived here. Her name was Christy. Lovely girl. Very lovely. Her mom took ill, something serious, cancer, yes, and didn't make it. As a single mom, her child Christy didn't have anywhere to go. Her mom was a good friend of mine, and she trusted me to take care of Christy.

"When Christy went to college, she had some influence that wasn't so desirable. Apparently, whatever that influence was, she cherished it. She stopped coming back here during holidays. Three years ago, I learned she was pregnant. But she still wouldn't come home. I felt terrible. I didn't even know where to find her. She stopped attending school.

"In the past three months, we have been in touch. She called. She is in a bad place. She lives with this man who, as best as I can tell, is a junky. She calls him her husband, but I bet they aren't married. The problem is, he beats her. First day she called me, she was in tears. I told her to come home. She agreed. Then he pleaded for her forgiveness. She called to say she wasn't returning anymore."

Grandma sighed. It was easy to see she was emotional over this.

"This routine has occurred several times in the last three months that she's been in touch. Today, she was supposed to get on a train and come down here, but when I called to ask if she was at the terminal, she asked me to forget it. Oh, the deja vu! The foolishness in this child! When I pressed her to get on that train, she accused me of being an enemy of love. This child is going to die and call it love?"

I felt grandma's pain. Even for me, I feel Christy's actions must be frustrating and indeed foolish. Why would she stay with someone who beat her up?

"Let me ask you something, child," she said. "I'm sorry if this is emotional for you, or tend to bring back memories, but it is necessary." I nodded. "Do you remember ever spending time with your dad?"

I nodded.

"Good. Do you believe your dad would beat you?"

That sounded ridiculous. "No."

"Why do you think so?"

"Because he loves me."

"Good. Good. And if he wanted you to have ice cream, would he ask which flavor you wanted?"

"Yes."

"Do you know why?"

"Why?"

"Because he respects you. He values your preferences." I nodded. "A man who raises his hand on you and does not care about your opinion, is not worth a moment of your time and attention. You must not tolerate that."

I nodded.

"You see, sometimes it's not only about the physical, whether he lays his hands on you or not. It could be through the demeaning things a man says to you. You mustn't tolerate unkind words from people."

I nodded. "I see why you were mad."

"I am fine now. You must let grandma return to her sewing okay."

"Okay. Bye, grandma."

"Yes, darling."

Going off to college was an interesting time for me. I looked forward to it. I knew it was a time to pursue the things I wanted most. The women back home were amazing, but I wanted to be a different woman. I wanted to weigh my own goals on different values. Being academically excellent and eventually making money were the things that mattered to me most.

I didn't want to be any man's woman. I thought nothing of a future with kids and being a great mother. I just wanted a life of wealth and luxury.

I was still convinced my choices were the best. I watched my best friend get beaten up until she was black and blue. I saw the things women faced—how they had no control over their lives or money; how their spouse or significant other controlled everything; how their world didn't just revolve around him, it was consumed by him. In the darkness of the moment, they hated him and themselves for allowing this treatment, but in the light of day, they wouldn't press charges or leave the relationship.

I couldn't understand. It was against what grandma taught me. I found myself resolving to never let anyone have that kind of control over me. Yes, I said *never*. When it came to submission, that was a gigantic wall that had to be torn down. I had to learn how to turn my strength into a blessing and not a hindrance in my marriage.

Just like I didn't want to be controlled, I couldn't control him as well. It couldn't be my way or the highway. My tears were not meant to be a means to manipulate, but a way of cleansing my soul of stress and pain. I had to also learn that my tears were not a sign of weakness, in a bad way, but another level of strength. It takes strength to be able to stand before God and/or your husband and be naked and unashamed knowing they can and will wipe away your tears. Not just wipe them away but bear the weight and be that support system that you can lean and depend on. Sometimes it takes more strength to be vulnerable and say I need help than to stand alone as a strong woman.

CHAPTER 4

"What will you have, ma'am?" the waiter asked us. He was a good looking guy, probably a student just like us. His attitude was carefree. One could tell he loathed the fact he had to wear a uniform.

It was a cheap restaurant. The owners tried as much as they could to make this less obvious, but it was a good-enough place for us. Trust me, most college kids would trade class for cheap. It was the second time Dasha and I were going there. It was Dasha's idea.

"Spaghetti and meatballs please," Dasha said. "And the same goes for her."

"Excuse me, lady, you don't tell me what to get," I said, serious.

Dasha turned to face me. "What would you have then?"

"Spaghetti and meatballs, of course."

"You clown!" I laughed. She turned to the waiter who managed a chuckle now. "Please."

"Be right back," he said and left.

Dasha and I met two weeks after I got into school. She bumped into me while looking for her class. Though she quickly apologized, it was easy to see she was confident. She spoke like she chose her words carefully, like she weighed their meaning and effect before letting them go. We started talking, and never stopped.

"Did you see that?" she asked me. "The way the waiter looked at you?"

"Oh please."

"You're blind to these things. It shouldn't be so."

"It seems to bother you, Dasha. Why?"

"I'm your best friend, if I let you wobble through school clumsily, what good have I done? How well will that speak of me?"

"Since this is about you and the reputation you're chasing, I'm sorry, I'll pass."

"Oh come on, AJ. All I'm saying is, give a guy a chance. Be involved with someone. Date. Kiss. Make love…" She laughed.

"Wo, wo! Slow down, young lady," I said.

"Not all in one day, calm down," she said, still laughing. "The thing is, if you don't let these experiences teach you, you won't learn. It is best to be experienced and then choose not to indulge. Ignorance isn't bliss. You ought to know."

She was right. I considered going out with a guy. When the waiter asked after our meal if he could have my number, I obliged.

Dasha smiled. "I knew today would be the first day you got yourself a boyfriend."

"He isn't my boyfriend, silly."

"It's only a matter of days, darling."

In a matter of days, we were dating. Dasha was so right, experience was good. Heartbreak was a learning curve. My first boyfriend was good at breaking hearts. It took him only three months to lose interest. I couldn't understand it.

"Well, he messed up, it isn't your fault," Dasha said to me when she saw how badly I was taking the breakup.

"How is it not my fault, Dasha? I gave him a chance into my life. I let him put me in this place."

"I understand," she said. "Don't we wish we had better instinct to help predict behaviors? But I can't watch you feel so bad about yourself over a guy that doesn't deserve it."

"You are trying to make me feel better. Don't."

"I am only speaking rationally, and yes, I want you to feel better. I'm your friend."

"Thanks."

"Your best friend."

"Thanks."

"The best you've got."

"Oh geez!"

She laughed. "Seriously, if anyone refuses to meet you in the middle, it's their problem. Not yours. Never yours."

Sometimes I thought Dasha was older than she was. Other times I felt she was a baby. She meant so much to me.

I gave dating another try. He was in my school, a bit of a geek, quiet and private. His name was Henry. He wasn't a particularly handsome guy—unlike the waiter. I felt it was safer to date a guy who wasn't so flashy, and who didn't suffer from lack of attentiveness.

"Tell me about Henry," Dasha said to me one afternoon. "No, not so much about him, but about you two."

"The only thing I can possibly tell you is, I found him myself. Not like that junk head you dumped on me."

"This is what I get for letting you understand men lie?" She sighed.

"I feel you haven't been punished enough," I told her.

"Oh come on, tell me about the two of you," she pleaded. "Is it going great?"

"It is, that's all you get." I left her.

It was only great for a while. Henry was the guy who treated me badly in subtle ways. He seemed to know how to maneuver me. He made me believe relationship could be about helping one another, and then he sneaked out. It was like he knew I would always come knocking. I had gotten used to him helping me fill a hole. I was stuck. He tormented me knowing how powerless I was.

When it was finally over, I didn't know how to feel. I felt like I lost my tormentor half the time, and other times, I felt I lost something close to a dad. In the end, I was left feeling terrible. I learned to trust men even less.

When I met Bellamy, I carried my skepticism into our affairs. There I was once again playing the role. Sure, I loved Bellamy with all my heart. Well, the parts that weren't shut down and locked away. Though I was now much older, the fear of being rejected and abandoned still gripped me. They made me question his loyalty to me. Deep down I didn't understand why he was with me. Everyone leaves at some point, so I always expected him to leave too. When I looked in the mirror, I didn't see the woman he saw. It would be years before I could look at old photos and see what he had always seen. I was beautiful... with my imperfections and all.

In the early weeks we began dating, I called Dasha and casually brought up Bellamy.

"Tell me about him," she said.

"Oh, there's nothing to tell. I'm sure it's nothing important."

She sighed. "AJ, if it was not important to you, you won't bring it up. I know a few things about you, just give me some credit. Now, tell me about this Bellamy guy."

"Well, he's a regular guy with a regular paid job. Office job. What isn't so regular about him is his attentiveness towards me. He pays so much attention it's troubling for me. He wants to know how I feel about everything. When I am talking about work activity, he listens with so much interest you'd think I was unveiling the world's best problem-solving technique to him."

Dasha laughed. "Yeah, I admit, it's troubling."

"I know, right?"

"Though, I must add that we create our own troubles."

"How so?"

"AJ, what I see here is you creating your own troubles, worrying about things that naturally should be positive. Have you now become so damaged or distrusting that you would define a great quality in a man as troubling?"

"Oh."

"If it was up to me, I'd say: allow this man to be attentive to you, allow him to treat you right. Get used to it. It is actually the way of life, not all the BS we got used to while growing up."

Dasha's words were golden. It restored some sense in me. However, more importantly, it left me uncertain. It made me want to hold onto and to keep Bellamy. I wasn't much of a keeper. I didn't know how. I forgot how to act around him. I was in unfamiliar territory.

In some areas, I was a go getter. As I got older, I found myself carrying the weight of the world on my shoulders. Apparently, this made it easier for me to mask the deeper issue of my insecurities. When I looked at the world, I could always find the rainbow, but when I looked introspectively it was so dark and cloudy. I excelled academically in the classroom but was afraid to walk through the doors that would open to me. There was always a crowd around me, but I felt alone most of the time.

There were so many opportunities I squandered not because I couldn't do it, but because I was afraid. I was a big, fat fraud. I looked and sounded confident, but I was far from it. There were so many things that I did just to say I could, but when it came time to do it on a consistent basis, I would graciously back away from the task.

I remember my senior year of college walking with my friend to talk to her advisor. When she was done, he turned to me and asked about my major, GPA, etc. I told him and he asked me to consider staying a few more semesters to take 3 classes that would give me a dual degree and set me up to apply for government jobs. As an African American female with those credentials I would have been set. I wouldn't have had to worry about a job because I had just helped get approval for the on-campus credit union. So many choices, but I never wanted to be in the lime light. I was content orchestrating from behind the curtain, never wanting to be on center stage. I was so accustomed to hiding in plain sight.

CHAPTER 5

B ack in college, after a few disappointments from the men-folk, Dasha and I made bullet point notes with the title—How To Tell If He Wants To Breakup. One of them stated: *if he was going to be late to a date but doesn't call beforehand; if he calls only while he is already late to the date; if he doesn't call at all but shows up much later only to spill a handful of excuses; he already is disregarding the relationship. At the very least, watch it, sis.*

Bellamy was thirty minutes late to our date! He never called to say he was going to be late; he never called while already late; he only came in all sweaty and harried. He looked like he had plenty to say, but all I saw was a man I'd rather not be talking to.

"I am so sorry," he said. I looked at him, letting my look do the talking. "It was not possible for me to be here earlier," he explained.

"Well, you're here now, how nice," I said. "You can have a seat, but I'm leaving anyway." I put my phone in my bag, ready to leave.

"At least, let me explain."

It sounded like the reasonable thing to do—hear him out. I settled back down. "Ok. Talk."

"I was at the hospital," he said. I was at once alarmed. "This neighbor, she was due. It seemed like she didn't know she was due. She didn't make plans. I was walking to my car so I could drive down here when I heard her calling from the window. She was obviously distressed. Well, long story short, I drove her to the hospital, made sure she was okay, before driving down. I could have called but I was a bit unsteadied by the whole thing and I couldn't afford to take my eyes off the road."

It was a good thing I listened to him, I told myself. It'd be cruel to get mad at a man who did what he did. If such led to a breakup, he'd always remember—and certainly not in a pleasant way—whenever I saw a pregnant woman.

"It's alright," I told him. "I'm sorry, too."

"Is it possible we can proceed with the date?"

"Yes, certainly. Though I have to leave in forty-five minutes. I have another engagement."

"Alright."

While we ordered and ate, his phone rang. It was his neighbor's boyfriend; he was calling to thank him for taking care of her. From then, I noticed Bellamy's attention was divided. He wasn't particularly distracted by anyone else or anything around us, he just seemed lost in thought. I thought it would be best to leave as soon as the meal was done with.

"Hey," he said.

"Yeah?"

"I've been thinking…"

"Obviously."

He sighed. "Do you want to have kids?"

That threw me off balance. At this time, Bellamy and I were fairly involved, but I hadn't expected our discussions to venture into things like that.

"I didn't mean to spring this on you," he said. "I guess it has to do with going to the hospital and seeing all those cute kids. You don't have to answer this."

Thank you! I told him I had to leave. He understood. He walked me to my car and planted a light kiss on my lips.

"You really look good," he said.

"Uh, you noticed."

He laughed. "Come on, I'd notice something so remarkably different in your dressing."

"How so?"

"You're wearing a dress, Amira. Usually, you'd do jeans and sneakers, or boots."

I managed a smile. "Do you like this more?"

"I like you in anything." He sounded like he meant it. "Though, I prefer you without a thing."

I blushed. "Silly. You won't make me miss my appointment." I kissed him on the cheek and got into the car. I liked that he stood there looking at me, his gaze unwavering, until I could no longer see him.

We never talked about kids anymore. However, two weeks after our engagement, I tactfully broached the subject. I believed I had the answer to his question.

"You remember that thing about kids, when you asked me. Do you want to ask me again?" I said.

He chuckled. "I have to ask again before you speak about it."

"I want to be certain it's something you want to talk about."

"Alright." He dropped his phone and turned to face me. "AJ, would you like to have kids with me?"

"That wasn't how you asked the question then."

He shook his head. "You can choose to answer how you like, there are no rules here."

I adjusted in my seat and took up my *serious talk posture.* "I was never the one to remember childbearing in my thoughts, my plans and all. Never thought big about it. I have to admit that has changed, though I can't tell to what degree. Sometimes you meet people and they make you think of other possibilities, they make you, without forcing you, assume new attributes. I think it's something I now look forward to, I mean having kids."

He nodded casually. "So, I'd be right to take the credit for changing you?"

"Is it that important to you?"

"In my art for example, a simple credit, like naming the songwriter of a song, can be a lot."

"I'm not giving you any credit," I said.

"If it means so much to you, that is, hanging on to the credit, then do so. I'll be fine."

"We are leaving the subject of this discussion behind. Petty."

He laughed now. I found myself joining him. "It's good. We will be good parents," he said. He drew me closer and kissed me. "I need you," he whispered into my ear.

"Go away, you're not getting me pregnant yet."

Like many young couples, we thought we would get married, have sex, get pregnant and have kids. Just one or two, not a lot. It wasn't supposed to be this hard. I had never even thought of the word infertility before, now I had to sit in the doctor's office answering questions that no person should have to answer. What was wrong with me? It was all my fault. Maybe if I hadn't made those statements about not wanting children growing up. What if I had been obedient instead of wrestling with God? What if I had…?

The emotional rollercoaster was the scariest ride I would ever have to take. Although the issue wasn't one hundred percent mine, I carried it around as one more thing I couldn't do right. At the mall, when I saw a pregnant woman, I thought to myself; that's yet another one. It was not easy managing my expectation and that of people.

Our inability to conceive consumed my mind so much that when Bellamy mentioned his office's mid-year dinner, I began to look forward to it. Any distraction from our predicament was welcome. I was beautifully dressed for the occasion. Bellamy was stylish in his navy blue suit. He introduced me to his colleagues, a few of whom I already knew.

One of them was particularly loud. "You are a most gorgeous, gorgeous woman," she said. Her name was Katrina Johnson.

"Thanks," I said. I was certain I didn't like her. I thought she used words carelessly.

"What are you wearing?" she asked.

"I don't know."

"How sad," she said and turned to Bellamy. "You know it's to your credit she's looking this gorgeous. You definitely have refused to have her belly budging." She giggled.

I was upset. It took the good nurturing in me to remove myself from there without causing a scene. Bellamy would later whisper to me that she was drunk.

Bellamy introduced me to Mr. Drew Jackson, the new director at their office. He was a gentle man. "I was at your wedding," he said. "I wasn't a director then. How long has it been? Two years, yeah, two."

"Well, congrats on your achievement," I said. "Bellamy has spoken of you a lot. The few times I was at the office, you were not anywhere to be seen."

"Bellamy is one of the good guys at the office," said Jackson. "I wonder if he feels he couldn't merge the two."

I looked at him. "What do you mean?"

"Oh, I mean doing a good job at the office and having kids. He should know it isn't as difficult as it seems. It's been two years, he should have figured that out already."

I can't understand why people get so worried when married couples don't have kids right away. It sucks, the whole nosing around and wise ass comments. I realized going to that event was a mistake.

"Excuse me," I said to Bellamy. I went out to the open terrace of the building. I needed fresh air. More importantly, I needed to be away from those clowns.

I was standing outside and thinking when someone cleared her throat beside me. Apparently I was going to bump into her without knowing it. "Oh, sorry," I said to her.

"It's alright."

She was wearing a big, beautiful black dress. The dress failed to hide her pregnancy. Another one, I said to myself.

"In need of fresh air?" she asked me.

"Yeah, yeah, fresh air. Umm, how are you?"

"I'm good. I'm guessing you don't know who I am."

"Not really."

"I work in the same office with your husband. My name is Evelyn Colin. I've seen you come to the office a few times."

"Oh. I'm Amira. Pleased to meet you." She nodded. "How far along are you?"

"Seven. It's going to be a girl."

I smiled at her. "How lovely." I liked her. "You're able to keep up at work well?"

"Sure."

"You're a strong woman. I hope I can be like you in my own time."

"I'm sure you will be." She smiled at me.

"Your first?"

She shook her head. "No. The first didn't stay though. Miscarried after four months. Darkest time in my life."

"I'm sorry," I said, wondering if I should ask her if losing the first had made her paranoid. I didn't. I was certain it'd make me just as nosy as the clowns inside the building.

"It's something. I'm ecstatic about this one but you always remember the first," she said. "It takes energy to keep going."

I felt for her. "I'm sure you'll be fine."

"Thank you…"

Bellamy burst out of the event hall. "Darling, we got to go," he said.

I knew not to question him. I could feel his feelings. I turned to Evelyn. "It was really nice meeting you. Hope to see you again."

"You, too, Amira. Hello, Bell."

"Hey," Bellamy said curtly. He grabbed me by the hand and we walked out.

In the car, I waited until we had driven for ten minutes before I asked him what was upsetting him. I expected he'd be calm enough to talk. I knew what the issue was, but it behoved on me to speak about it.

"How exactly is it their problem?" he spat. "I mean, whether we have a kid yet or not, whether we will be having or won't, really, how is that any of their problem? Suddenly, they all have a say. Oh Bell, it's been two years! Oh Bell, how come you're killing time? Dear Lord, give me the grace not to grab someone and smash their head against the wall."

I was sad. Bellamy was suffering. It was never the greatest news when the doctors say you might be suffering from low sperm count. I had literally spent all my internet time looking up low sperm count, causes, symptoms, remedies. This subject was even more taboo than a woman that was unable to conceive. I didn't have the words to console Bellamy. Like him, I also lacked the patience to deal with the annoying people that wouldn't mind their own business. Whenever they asked, I felt a dagger stab into my heart. In my head it played out like those scenes from a movie where the person is standing there with a blank stare but in their mind, there is another conversation taking place that involved yelling, screaming and throwing things at their head. They meant well, but they had no idea the struggles we were going through.

I reached out and put my hand on Bellamy's thigh. I hoped he understood that I was with him, and that I understood what he was going through.

When he pulled up at the house, he turned the engine off and turned to me. "Maybe there's a way of going about this. The most important is not to be angry when people ask these questions, because they won't stop asking."

"Why the hell would we need to do that?" I asked.

He frowned. "Huh?"

"Look at it this way. We owe no one nothing. We don't need to adjust our feelings for anyone when we could just cut them off."

Bellamy thought about it, and then began to nod. "Yeah, yeah, cut them off. Avoid their circle, yeah."

"Good."

I longed to be a mom, but it didn't seem to be on the cards. The last thing I needed was people reminding me of it. It was on my mind all the time.

"Let's go in," Bellamy said with this look I couldn't describe.

Once the door was closed, he grabbed me and pressed me against the wall. He was all over me, touching, smooching, kissing and licking. He was wild. My breath came in gasps. He lifted me onto the table and made love to me. Maybe it was the anger he felt earlier, maybe it was something else only he understood, but it was the first time in a long time that we enjoyed lovemaking. Sex had ceased being a pleasurable ride for us. After the strips, shots, pills, and charts, perhaps you'd understand why this became the case. There was always an agenda to it... a goal that was to be met, yet not met. Sadly, after that night, we couldn't rekindle that spark again. We went back to what we were.

I carried with me an extra burden. The doctor's thoughts about my chances were not the best. When I get pregnant, I'd have to be careful during that period because I was predisposed to some health problems. A c-section would be in order as well to ensure a safe delivery for me and the baby. One more reason to hate the skin I was in. My hips were not built for childbirth.

Bellamy watched more football games. The live show, the recaps, the highlights, the prediction games. He didn't watch them with the passion with which he did when we were still dating. He saw them now as a way of distracting himself from the issues.

"You haven't been yourself in a long time," I said to him one morning as I drank a cup of coffee. He said nothing. He just sighed. "And you hardly speak."

"Trust me, I've been saying a lot."

I frowned. "You have? I must be the one hallucinating."

"You're not."

"It must be you then."

"AJ, no one's hallucinating. I just have been talking in my head more."

"Do you care to talk to me about what you've been talking to yourself about?" He just sat there in bed for a while, not speaking. I stood by impatiently. "Look, Bellamy…"

"There is no easy way to go about it, AJ. It's typically more questions than answers. Like, what will happen if we don't get a breakthrough? Like, how are we handling this; are we even going about it the right way? There's just this pressure, and every day I feel I am sinking under. And you, too, I feel you're going under. We are just…" He cut off and looked away. "We just seem to be incapable of lifting each other."

"That's what you've been talking about?"

"There are fragments and fragments of these things. It's just difficult to put them into a concise form."

"Maybe we wouldn't be so incapable of lifting each other if you talked to me more."

"I didn't think in our predicament I have exonerated myself in any way. Obviously, I can't even do that, given a chunk of the issue rests on me. But to have blames easily shifted to me, wow, I didn't see that coming."

"Why do I sense you're playing the victim here?" I asked, getting upset.

"I'm not playing. It's not a game for me. Don't know if I can say the same for you."

"What do you mean?"

He left the room and walked into the living room. He sat heavily on the couch, his face furrowed. I was right there, standing over him, agitated. "I asked you a question, Bellamy. What do you mean?"

He kept mute.

"What the hell do you mean? Have you become an invalid around your vocal cord? I take the news of the conditions—yours and mine—and I incubate it all, I persist with you, searching for solutions and all that, yet you sit here and insinuate I might be insensitive. How dare you?"

He met my gaze. "Now you're going to put words into my mouth?"

"If you didn't infer that, then what the hell do you mean?"

"That's it right there. That's the problem."

"What's the problem?" I was almost yelling.

Bellamy was calm. "That's it. The pushing. The consistent pressing. When we talk about our situation, all I feel is you on the other side; asking me questions I have no answers to, pressuring me. You don't say it, but I feel it. It's as if each time you talk to me you're trying to find out if I have a timeline for our condition—maybe mine, yeah, my condition—to be fixed."

I was shocked. "Jesus Christ! I don't do that!"

He rose now. "You have no idea how much you do," he said calmly. "You can't even let me see a game. I was once seeing a high profile football game, you came over and stood in front of the TV. You asked me if we would need to increase our schedule with the doctor. At the very moment I'm watching a game! And I won't be allowed that respect!"

My jaw dropped. I didn't know what to say to him.

"The thing is, that day, I looked at you for a long time standing in front of the TV. I was certain you didn't realize you were standing in front of the TV. You didn't know. That's how much the pressure has become." With that said, he picked up his car keys and left the house.

I had no idea things were eating Bellamy up from the inside. I certainly had no idea I had inadvertently been contributing to his worries. I wasn't sure he was right. Also, I was not sure he knew exactly how much he was hurting me as well. I thought of us all the time and it was killing me inside. I needed Bellamy to talk things through with me. I didn't want him to solve our problem all by himself, I just wanted to talk. He didn't help.

Further visits to the hospital presented scarier news. Apparently, I was not the safest person to carry a baby in my womb. The doctor said the risk was something to be concerned about. Bellamy was even more frustrated.

"What's even the point?" he said one evening during dinner.

"What are you talking about?"

He took my hand in his. "I don't want anything to happen to you."

I sighed. I was worried as well. "I think I'll be fine," I said to him, trying to sound brave.

"I can't forgive myself."

"You mustn't think that way, Bellamy."

He nodded. Then he returned to his food. The spoon remained stuck in his hand. He couldn't eat anymore.

"You okay?" I asked.

"We are trying to conceive. We are doing all we can. In the end, it's not even safe for you. How crueler can it get?"

The thought of losing me was etched in Bellamy's brain. He was scared to death. Every day was like a horrible episode of Oprah's favorite things. I felt his lips quiver when I kissed him. Bellamy was right; it was cruel. We were denied everything. Sexual pleasure was eluding us as well. Out in the park, on the bus, everywhere; you see them. Babies! Everybody got a baby except Bellamy and AJ. Some girls would look at a guy and wind up pregnant; the ones that ignore using birth control and would readily choose to have an abortion. I know that sounds melodramatic because so many other families struggle with this issue daily, but you get the point.

Bellamy and I couldn't save ourselves from drifting apart. It was becoming painful living through this. Our conversations became short and very tense. It was like walking around on eggshells. A carefree moment would leave us clashing. Daily, we were becoming more like roommates than husband and wife. The situation literally choked the life out of our relationship. The worst part was, I had no idea how to stop it.

Remember that strong woman from earlier? Well, I no longer felt safe or loved. My words were sharp while his were crass and our timing was completely off. This man was my best friend, my safe place full of joy and laughter. Now, all that was left was a hard shell that I couldn't crack.

Why would I feel the need to have a major conversation during the championship game of the basketball final four or the Superbowl? I know. I know. That is the absolute worst time to try and talk to any guy about anything other than what he wants to eat or drink. At the time though, it seemed like an opportune time because he seemed happy. I was trying to maximize the moment.

The infertility and communication breakdown would aid in the creation of the perfect storm.

CHAPTER 6

I was a bit of a late bloomer. While most girls were chasing boys, I had my nose in a book. I'm pretty sure you get this much already, but just don't know why it was so for me. I was born to a teenage mom, so I was determined not to be another statistic. It isn't like I wasn't showered with love, but I wasn't in mom's plan. I just happened. She was stuck with having to have me.

I accomplished my goal, but I missed out on a lot of flirting and learning what boys and men were like. I was like a fish out of water. If Dasha hadn't come along when she did, I might still have been in that water.

The second reason, which I never shared with anyone but Dasha, was because of the way I was raised.

"Why is God watching me?" I asked grandma one evening while she made a simple dress for me. This question was a precipitate of her incessant 'God is watching'. I was twelve then.

"For two reasons," she said. "To protect you, because he is a loving father. And the other is, he takes account of your actions. When you do wrong things, sinful things, he is aware, and he isn't happy about those."

This stuck with me. It impacted what I did and didn't do. I didn't feel the way my friends did about sex. I'm not saying I was a virgin and I really enjoyed when it happened, but it was something I wasn't comfortable embracing. There were a million things in my mind, sex was of the least priority.

For some reason, in my head, marriage didn't change that fact. Maybe because we weren't taught that the marriage bed was undefiled. So much time was spent preaching to the singles that no one was ministering to the couples.

Once I shifted from religion to relationship, pleasing God and my pastor became my number one goal and sometimes that meant not pleasing my husband. I was so engulfed with ministry in the church building that I was neglecting my first ministry at home. I was so out of order. Bellamy would look at me and wonder where this "church lady" came from because that wasn't the person that used to tease him in the restaurant or take him from zero to ninety with a glance.

As a married woman, it took me a while to separate the Woman of God from the wife. There were times he needed me to simply be the scripture by wrapping my arms and legs around him and covering him and making *him* feel safe. Allowing him to lay his head in my lap and speak freely. When he came through the door the noise could cease, and he knew he was home. I didn't have to fix everything or be his conscience. I had to be his safe place… a confidant… his helper. This didn't come naturally to me, but a lesson I had to learn if I was going to have a long and prosperous marriage.

Grandma would say, when you leave a problem unsolved, it pretty much grows and brings other problems with it. This became my situation with Bellamy.

I went to his office to see him. This wasn't out of the ordinary. Normally would drop by the office if I wasn't too busy, or if I took the day off.

"Hey, honey," Bellamy said when he saw me. "You didn't say you were dropping by."

"I was told you liked surprises," I said.

"No one told you that."

I laughed. "Care to swing by a restaurant for lunch?"

"Umm…" Bellamy stalled, thinking about it.

I looked beyond his cubicle and saw Evelyn. "Oh, Evelyn is back from her maternity leave," I said to Bellamy.

"Yeah, yeah, she's back. Been about three months. Didn't I mention it to you?"

"I'm sure I'd have remembered that. I want to go over and say hi."

"Sure."

I walked over to Evelyn's cubicle. She smiled brightly when she saw me. "Amira! Oh, look at you!"

I hugged her. "You look great," I said to her. I meant it. "I didn't know you were back. How is your little daughter?"

"She's great. Though I can't stop calling the caregiver every twenty minutes." She laughed.

We talked for a couple of minutes until I was distracted. Some lady in cubicle three was with Bellamy. She knew how to throw her long, wavy hair just at the right moment as she giggled and brushed her hand on Bellamy's forearm. She laughed at his joke and hung on every word that fell from his beautiful lips. I could see she was attentive to him.

Evelyn followed my line of sight. "Oh, that's Janie," she said to me. "Been with us for five months."

"That's her name? I've seen her before, but not like this."

"Like what?"

I turned to Evelyn. "Is it me, or is she flirting with my husband?" Evelyn opened her mouth and closed it. "Talk to me, Evelyn," I said.

"Flirting? I wouldn't be so sure of that," she said. "I think perhaps she's just a nice person. It's reflected in the lunchbox she hands out. She has…"

I frowned. "She brings him food?"

"Not all the time. It may be nothing serious."

"And it could be something."

"I don't know what to say."

"I'm sorry to have bothered you. It's good to see you again," I said to her. "I have to go now."

"Alright," she said, managing to produce a bright smile. "Pleased to see you again as well. Bye."

I returned to Bellamy. Janie was gone. He looked up. "Honey, you just missed Janie, my colleague."

"I see."

"She had this pasta made for me," he said, smiling. "Isn't she nice?"

I looked at him. What a fool he was. He was oblivious to what was going on. He couldn't see the twinkle in her eye, the curve of her back, but I could. Not a jealous wife talking, I saw these things.

"I take it I drove down here for nothing then," I said.

He looked concerned. "No, honey, I'm pleased you came. We can go out for lunch. I'll just get a drink."

"Forget it."

"You okay?"

"I'm perfect."

"That's good then."

Again, what a fool! Did no one teach him no wife was okay seeing her husband get fed by another woman. In the coming weeks, I called Evelyn more. We spoke about her baby and how she was coping with the stress. More importantly, I brought up Janie and my husband.

He was still getting lunch boxes from her. While he ate, they talked. What I heard was—she listened to him all the time without judging. It seemed they were talking for longer minutes. It seemed he laughed more around her. I could see why. With her, he had no baggage to carry—something that had since eluded our relationship.

"What do you mean when you said she touched him?" I asked Evelyn one evening after work, sitting up on the couch.

"Not in any inappropriate way or…"

"In what way was it?" My chest was beating fast.

"In that gentle, sweet little way," you know. "Like holding hands, but in a very delicate way."

Oh God! "Were they talking when she touched him?" I asked.

"Umm…"

"You need to remember."

"I don't know why that's important. They talk a lot."

"I just need to know."

"Uh… yeah, I think, yes, they were talking."

I felt weak. The gentle touch. The sweet words—so different from mine. I was losing my husband's attention.

"Thank you, Evelyn," I said. "We will speak again." I hung up.

Bellamy and I barely talked now. I could tell talking to me had become like talking to his mother. He now had a fine lady to draw comparisons with. I knew I was coming up short. I had his heart, I was his wife, but she was in his ear. How long would that last for me?

CHAPTER 7

"Are you happy with yourself?" I asked Bellamy one evening, my tone confrontational.

He looked up from his phone, his face furrowed. "What are you talking about?"

"Other people would go to work and then return home. I mean, really return home. But for you, you're trying to make your workplace your home. Great."

"Again, AJ, what are you talking about?" he looked genuinely confused now.

"You know. You know what you're doing."

"Tell me, or leave me the hell alone."

I was taken aback. Then I thought I would be even more bitter if I allowed him to pretend through all this. "It's about you and Janie! Are you going to deny it now?"

He looked at me, horrified. "What is with you?"

"The talking, the lunch boxes, the touching…"

"What touching?"

"What's next for you two? What's next, huh?"

"Oh God, don't start, AJ!"

"I didn't start nothing, you started it all. What is she now? Your soulmate? Your work wife? Are the two of you going to take it up a notch?"

"Something is wrong with you, AJ."

"Something is wrong, and it's not me."

He was quiet for a while, like his energy had leaked away. I wondered if my words had hurt him.

"AJ," he said finally. I felt relieved he was talking again. "Janie and I are just friends. She has been through a lot. She just talks things over with me. We have no intention of having a relationship. I am married. She knows that. Please, don't start something where there is nothing."

He walked away. *Something is wrong, and it's not me.* I know that was not the best thing to say to a man struggling to come to terms with his issues. But in that moment, I was more occupied with what was going on between him and Janie. I went into the bathroom and called Evelyn.

"Hey, Mira," she said when she took the call. Her baby was crying in the background. I felt bad bothering her at that moment, but I didn't drop the call.

"Hey, I want to run something by you."

"Go on."

"Janie, did she go through something? Like some sort of misfortune or something."

"Not that I know of."

"Bellamy mentioned that. So I was wondering if it is in the public domain."

"I might have known if it was in the public domain."

"Ok. One more thing please." I could hear the baby wailing, but I fired on anyway. "I want to know…"

"Hey, Amira, I'm really sorry, I got to go." She hung up.

I felt ashamed. I should have hung up and called her back later. I sighed and dialed Dasha's number. She picked up after the second ring.

"Do you miss me so much, girl?" she asked, laughing loudly. It was obvious she was in a good mood.

Dasha and I had remained friends after school. Now we worked in the same organization. Though she was married with two kids, we still treated each other like college kids.

"Dash, I just confronted Bellamy over the time he spent with Janie at the office."

"Confronted? I remember saying you could have a discussion with him about it, not confront."

"I tried. I couldn't manage a quiet, mature talk."

She sighed. "With confrontation, people tend to achieve less. Anger gets in the way. Unintended words get said, and the issue escalates. Anyway, what came out of this. I'm sure you're calling to tell me."

"He said they're just friends, and that Janie had been through a lot. So she talks it over with him."

"And?"

"Nothing else, except the fact that that worries me. I mean, if he is burdened with the issues we have here and she's been through a lot, isn't that usually the recipe from which two people fall for each other?"

"I see what you mean. You are not too wrong. But what will determine what happens now is what you do next."

"What should I do next?"

"You either pull him in and become the friend he sees in Janie, or just keep being the wife he is currently seeing in you."

"I don't think he is seeing a great wife in me currently."

"My point exactly."

"He needs to come to me as well," I said. "I have to feel needed. Valued. Important."

"Those, too."

I could hear her husband, Dom yelling her name in the background. I did the right thing this time. "Thanks for this, Dash. I got to go."

"Take it in, boo." She hung up.

I took a cold shower. By the time I was done, I resolved I didn't have to try to please Bellamy. If he had chosen to find warmth outside our union, then that's his problem. I needed him and he wasn't there. Sure, physically, I saw him every day, but emotionally there was not a connection. I believe in communication and tackling things head on, but if things persist, I tended to relieve pressure in other ways.

I've felt rejected and abandoned a lot in my life. I was feeling it again with Bellamy. I know it might not have been his intention, but I was a slave to my feelings. When he made no attempt whatsoever to reach out to me, to talk more, to find me, what exactly was he telling me?

I found myself in that place again where I would cling on to anyone or anything that made me feel safe. I grew up in the Neo Brown era (New Jack City), if you didn't give me what I wanted I would just hit cancel and get another.

I know that is not the attitude of a good Christian woman, but I wasn't always the good Christian woman. So, when these situations persisted and his attention was elsewhere, I found safety and security in the eyes and arms of another. Nope it was not the Lord.

I was at one of my favorite restaurants when I met her. I heard her talking from a corner of the restaurant. Her voice was smoky. I was drawn to listen to it. It wasn't just the voice, but what she was saying and how she was saying it. I imagined the confidence of such woman. I rose, having just finished my meal and settled the bill, and walked toward the corner where she was sitting. There she was, slim, busty, and with a face that couldn't be more oval. It was easy to see how tall she was.

I didn't know how hard I was staring, and how reluctant I was to stop until her eyes met mine. She waved me over with a smile. I went to her. She was sitting with a man.

"Sit please," she said once I was over at the table. As soon as I sat down, she stretched her hand. I presented mine. She shook it firmly. "I am Tiffany," she said.

"Amira," I said. "Good to meet you."

"This here is Charlie, an old acquaintance of mine," she said, introducing the man opposite her. "Hey," I said.

"Nice to meet you," Charlie said. "I was just leaving though." He rose.

"Yes, he was just leaving," Tiffany said. "See you soon, Charlie."

"Alright. Bye. Take care, girls."

I waved and watched him leave. I turned to face Tiffany. I didn't know what I was doing there. It felt awkward. "I thought you have a great voice," I said, hoping it would get less awkward.

"African," she said.

"What?"

"I sound like Africans, I've been told."

"Oh. I wouldn't know."

"It's not entirely true though. I've been there. A lot of the people I met there don't sound like me."

"What's Africa like? I've once flirted with the idea of visiting one of the countries up north."

"The real Africa is down south. My opinion. And for me, Africa is fascinating. It shows you a hell of a whole lot of things you didn't know."

"Wow! I always thought that."

Tiffany sipped from her glass. "I was in Guinea... Want anything?"

"No. I just finished at the table further down."

"Okay. Anyway, I was in Guinea. We had come into this bush bar for pepper soup and goat meat. They love pepper in Africa. It's their biggest spice. So, while we were waiting for our orders, I noticed this woman, perhaps in her mid-forties. She was sitting a few tables away from us. She was dressed in this colorful, exotic dress. Two men were sitting beside her, eating pepper soup from the same plate while she ate from a different plate. She had a presence that sort of got you looking.

"The waiter caught me looking at her. Without asking, he chose to tell me about the woman. Her name was Madam Abide. She was a dancer. The two men beside her were her husbands."

"Oh my God!" I exclaimed.

"I know, right. What fascinated me about Madam Abide was how humble and cooperative her two husbands were. Isn't Africa something?"

"Definitely." I laughed.

"I got to learn Madam Abide had announced she would be taking another husband the following year, and that her two husbands were tasked to find someone fitting. Though, if she wanted, she could find one herself. But it was always better the two men found another they were certain they could live with."

I laughed like I hadn't in a long time. "Fascinating. OMG! Incredible!"

We talked for a long time. And then it was few minutes past 7:00 P.M. We had finished a bottle of wine by now, and Tiffany had smoked seven or eight cigarettes. "You think we should head home?" she asked.

"Absolutely."

"Charlie drove me here," she said. "You think you can drive me back?"

"Sure."

We got up and left the restaurant. On the drive to Tiffany's, I couldn't help but recognize how much I enjoyed talking to her. It was so easy, engaging and fascinating. At thirty-one, she was a woman with a lot of experience.

When I pulled up at the front of her house, she asked if I wanted a glass of water. I said, yes. I didn't want to drink water,

I was sure. I wanted to see her apartment. We walked to the door, and she opened it. Interestingly, her apartment was simple. It lacked all the elements of the exotic tales she told.

She got me a glass and watched me drink. "Want to see something on TV? A show perhaps?"

"I think I should be heading back," I said.

"Alright." She walked me to the door, but instead of opening it, she pushed my back against it. Then she pressed her body against mine and kissed me. There was a hunger in the way she kissed. She probed and found my tongue, and sucked.

I kissed back. I didn't know why. I just kissed.

"I've been wanting to do that for months," she said. Then she stepped back, breathing. "Good night," she said.

I opened the door and left. My legs were shaky as I made it to my car. I kept thinking of her on the way home. Her voice, her stories, her kiss...

Wait a minute! What did she mean when she said she'd been waiting to do that for months?

For the next two days, I thought of Tiffany. She was such a mystery to me. On the third day, at around 7:00 P.M., I found myself driving over to her apartment. She let me in after I knocked on her door.

"I have two questions," I said as soon as I stepped into the room.

"That's fine," she said calmly. "But not before a drink."

"I don't want a drink," I said.

"Please."

I sat down. "Okay." I wondered what her plan was. Get me drunk and then kiss me again?

She brought the drink. "It's tea, made from root. The most calming tea you'd ever try," she said.

Tea? I was sure she wouldn't stop leaving me marveled. I took the cup from her. "Thanks." I drank patiently while she sat on a couch. When I was done, I said to her; "Two things."

"I'm listening," she said.

"When did you find out you were a lesbian?"

"Since college. It started with me finding out I preferred a woman's kiss. The more girls I kissed, the less I wanted to kiss boys. When did you find out about yourself?"

"I am not…"

"I know." She looked at me, and I could tell she was thinking of the many things she could do to me.

"My second question. What did you mean when you said you've been wanting to kiss me for months?"

"I meant just that."

"Months?"

"Months."

"You just met me."

She looked at me, frowning. Then she laughed. "You really don't know me?"

"I don't. Am I supposed to?"

"We attend the same church."

"Oh my God! We do? We really do?" I was worried.

"Yes. Sure." I felt ashamed. I had just let a church member kiss me. "I can tell why you wouldn't know me though," she said.

"Why's that?"

"I just get in there, and I'm out. Not a worker like you."

"You really know me."

She smiled. "I hope to know you better."

She made me calm down. Or, perhaps the tea took effect. She told me about her life. I found myself telling her about mine. She was easy to talk to and she understood everything I was going through. She didn't try to kiss me, or touch me. Just before 9:00 P.M., she walked me to my car and said bye.

We had a few more innocent girl outings. We went to a club once and danced until I felt my heart pound. She was eccentric. She made me do new things, and I loved them. I found myself always looking forward to seeing her.

One evening, she invited me over to her place. When she brought her lips close to mine, I was already in need of her. I kissed her. I pushed her onto the couch. When she reached below and felt me, she smiled.

"You shaved," she said, her voice husky as well.

I was slightly shy. I liked this woman. I hadn't planned to be with a woman, or ever given it a thought, but here I was.

"I have desired you for so long," she whispered into my ears.

Honestly, I thought I was undesirable to anyone but Bellamy. So, when I began to have these feelings, I was just as shocked. I began to feel something that I had never felt before for anyone. All our jokes about Jodie sneaking in the house took on a new meaning. I am not making light of anyone's story or situation but shedding light on something that happens more often than you think. It has been around for years and is still hiding in plain sight. I was vulnerable and hurt and for the first time in a long time, I felt safe.

One Saturday afternoon, Tiffany and I were in her kitchen making fish stew when she said; "You know, the flight to Gao International Airport might be bumpy—pretty much likely because the weather forecast might be slightly off, but Gao promises nice meals. The fonio and roasted capitaine fish would blow your mind in an incredible way. I've tried making those here using the recipe I found online, but I couldn't quite get it right. More importantly, the adventure is all the adrenaline you need."

I frowned. "What are you talking about?"

"I feared you may ask that. I'm proposing a trip."

"You are? Girl, are you crazy!"

She laughed. "Gao is just a bus drive from Timbuktu. And you already know…"

"Where are all these places you're mentioning?"

"Gao? Timbuktu? I really have to take you to school, don't I?" She sniggered. "Well, they are in Mali. Timbuktu was amongst the world's biggest civilization in the fourteenth and fifteenth century. Though mostly a shadow of itself, but it's still pretty historic."

"Timbuktu huh?" I said.

"Used to be home for this big library where world people came to do important research. Hard to believe huh? Africa!" she sighed. "But the adventure begins with understanding that since 2012, the country has had major political disruptions by the Tuareg rebels. Imagine holidaying in a place you can't guarantee as stable. Pretty cool, right? Adrenaline will be all over the place." She laughed and tossed spices into the pot.

"I'd rather consider traveling to Europe first," I said.

"Playing it safe, huh? Europe is predictable. Have you seen a man dancing with crocodiles before? You won't see that in Europe."

I sighed. "If we are going to take our first trip, let's start on relatable footing."

"Fine," she said reluctantly.

We were opposites in many ways, but we worked. There was not any competition. Of course I wasn't going to Africa with her, but I couldn't deny she brought something new to my life. I looked forward to the new crazy stuff she was into.

Bellamy and I were getting ready to leave the house for work. He said casually; "I couldn't help but notice you are out often."

I said nothing. I felt I didn't owe him an explanation. It wasn't like he had done something about his friendship with Janie.

I kissed him lightly on the cheek. "Have a good day," I said and left the apartment.

When we returned from work, I told him I wanted to go on a trip the following week. He looked at me for a long time, and then shook his head.

"It seems you have made plans to travel alone," he said eventually.

"Yes."

"Where?"

"Italy. Florence mostly."

"Okay."

I went on the trip with Tiffany. It was the craziest trip I ever took. She made me wear butt hugging, thighs-exposing bum shorts in the street. I drank more than I ever did in my entire life. We were loud and lavish at the club. Back at the hotel, we made explosive love and got ready for another day of adventure.

When I returned, things were different in the house. Bellamy began spending less and less time at home. He preferred the studio more. He channeled his energy there, doing more and more songs, collaborations, and even pitching to be a part of a touring group of artists.

It didn't affect me. Tiffany was a handful, and I felt pretty occupied. In the house, Bellamy and I talked like two civilized roommates would. Lovemaking was hardly ever in our routine. One evening however, he was sitting in the living room when I entered. I was late again.

"Can we talk as soon as you can manage?" he said.

"Sure," I said, and walked into the room. I took my time. When I returned to the living room, it seemed he hadn't moved an inch from his position.

"My friendship with Janie had bothered you for months now," he said. "I didn't feel it would be a threat to our marriage. I was wrong."

I kept looking at him. I thought he was beginning to figure out I was away from the house more as a protest against their friendship. I waited.

"I was wrong about a lot of things. I was so certain Janie wanted nothing from me. I was shocked when she made a pass on me."

I looked sharply at him with furrowed face.

"Yes, she told me she wanted me. She actually did try to caress me when we were alone. She had told me her car was faulty, and at the end of the day, she needed help getting home. I opted to drive her. That's what friends do, right? I didn't know it was a ploy to get me to be sexually involved with her."

"What did you do?" I asked, my voice sharp.

"Nothing. I shrugged her off, told her I was married, and I wanted it to remain that way."

I could feel myself breathing again. It was obvious I loved Bellamy. I didn't want him to fall into some other woman's lap.

"I am sorry," he said. "I should have been suspicious. You told me. I thought you were being irrational. It is safe to say now that our friendship is over."

"Okay," I said.

"I know you've been so distant from me because of her. I'm sorry. You don't need to be distant anymore."

He was wrong. It wasn't because of Janie. It was because I wanted someone. Tiffany became available. I wasn't going to cast her away. I liked her.

I continued to see Tiffany. Bellamy didn't talk much about it. After some weeks, he began to make insinuations. And then, much later, it turned into a full blown out argument.

"You don't care about my feelings," he roared.

"Your feelings?" I said, unperturbed.

"You thought I'd feel awesome that my wife wouldn't spend time with me? She'd rather just walk in whenever she wanted and walked straight to bed?"

"I work a lot, I get tired, and all I want to do is rest."

"What a weak alibi! You could have tried."

"It's not a lying game," I said. "It's a game of facts, and I have stated the facts."

"What bothers me is you're not even trying to find tangible excuses." He stormed off.

I laid in bed thinking; this man has to give me a break, period.

"Ma'am, there's someone at the reception to see you," the receptionist called to inform me.

"Who?"

"Wouldn't give her name. Says she'll need you to come down."

"That's insane."

"Should I call security?"

I thought about it. "No, I'm coming."

It was Tiffany. She had a huge smile on her face when she saw me. I didn't know how to react. I mean, me and this woman get naked in bed and do things to ourselves, I couldn't possibly know what to say to her in such formal environment.

"I've got this," I said to the receptionist. I produced a warm smile to Tiffany. "Come into my office."

Once the door was closed, I said; "You could have given me a heads up."

"And miss the look on your face when you saw me? Nah."

"You and your little games."

"I was missing the heck out of you," she said. "I haven't seen you in two days."

"That's a lot of time, huh" I said.

"That sarcasm." She drew me closer and kissed me. I felt weak around the knees and sat on the table. She slid her hand into my skirt.

"Oh God, not here!"

"It will be crazily sweet, you'll see," she said.

"No."

"I am disappointed." She looked disappointed.

"I will be over after work."

"It's a date. Come with you're A-game." She winked. Then she turned and left.

I took a deep breath.

Later that evening when I arrived home, Bellamy was waiting.

"Who is Tiffany?" he asked.

I was shocked. I couldn't hide it. "Why?" I managed. I was certain I had been found out.

"She was here about twenty minutes ago. Said she couldn't get you on the phone."

"Oh, I sent my phone for repair."

"Who is she?"

"Umm… ah… my friend."

"How come I don't know her? I thought I knew all your friends. She even knows the house, but I don't know her."

"She is a bit of a new friend."

"I see." I thought Bellamy might be suspicious. I didn't know what to do to make him not be. "You have been on the phone with her a lot lately," he said. "Tiff, isn't it?"

"Yeah. Yeah. We are also in the same church."

"Huh."

After two weeks, Bellamy was back to pestering me. He asked; "What's really going on with you and Tiffany?" My heart beat fast. Had Tiffany been talking to Bellamy. "She was here again to see you," he said. "She looked like she had to see you at once. If it wasn't an emergency, then she had to be on drugs. The way she behaves…"

"Hey, don't talk like that about my friend." My voice was sharp. I pretended I was angry so as to avoid answering his question.

"Do you know Jodi?" he asked.

"Who's Jodi?"

"Jodi Xabi, an old friend. Remember we ran into him at the airport once. Short, chubby, and talks too much."

"I don't." I didn't care to remember Jodi. My heart was beating too fast to be concerned about his talkative friend.

"He told me he ran into you at a party."

What now? I thought.

"You were with a woman. When I asked him to describe this woman, he described Tiffany. So, what's up?"

I thought fast. It was easier to go with the obvious truth. "Yeah, we were bored one evening and ended up at the party. Nothing much."

"I see," he said. "For church people like you two, that is more than slightly eccentric."

That night, I thought being with Tiffany was becoming difficult for me. It wasn't just that I had begun to feel guilty whenever I saw Bellamy unhappy, I had also begun to feel uncomfortable with Tiffany. She wanted more than I could give. She wanted me to leave Bellamy and take a trip with her. She wanted me to live free and wild like her—quit my job and go to Africa or India or South America. Crazy stuff. She said I was addictive. That's crazy. She demanded my attention, and she couldn't be trusted to respect my space. She invaded everywhere.

It was getting harder and harder to keep the lies straight. I found myself answering questions. *Why was Tiffany always leaving voice messages? Did she say she was missing you?*

I saw myself as someone with many faces. Bellamy, Tiffany, work, and church all got a different side of me. I was the master at compartmentalizing. Tiffany was ruining it all.

I got a call from the manager to come into his office. I went. "Is something going on?" he asked.

"No, everything is fine."

"The guys we are talking to are yet to get a call from you, and it's been forty-eight hours."

I forgot. I meant to give them a call. I had no excuse. I told the manager it must be the migraine. It wasn't that.

I was literally living hell on earth and my home was ground zero. I was numb. I would sit in church service like a zombie. Sure, I smiled, but life had completely lost its purpose and focus. I wanted to die and several times I came really close to going through with it. I had hurt and betrayed the person that I loved most in the world, turned my back on my faith, and didn't recognize the woman that was looking at me in the mirror. I was disgusted with myself and life... there was no hope. The light had gone out in my eyes.

I woke up one morning and began to cry. It dawned on me how much I was hurting my husband. It became very vivid how far I had strayed from the ways I was brought up. It left me sober. I had lost my personal relationship with God. I felt he couldn't hear me anymore. And now I was not performing at my best at my workplace.

I began to cry. I cried until Bellamy found me. I didn't tell him why I cried. He let me cry. Then he brought me coffee.

"I'm fixing breakfast," he said.

That security I felt I had was short-lived because it was built on a lie that would come crashing down around me for many reasons. I was far from fulfilling God's will for my life. The doors of my heart were opened, and the years of pain came gushing out. My body was overwhelmed and went into overload. All I could do was sit and cry. My thoughts were all over the place.

Bellamy announced that breakfast was ready. We ate together for the first time in a while. I thought while we ate, that everything I wanted was right in front of me. All I had to do was claim it, and be good to it. But it was already too late.

That evening, I went to Dasha's house. She was worried when she saw me at the door. I hadn't given any notice I was coming over. She took one look at me, and knew I was a mess.

"Oh dear," she said. "Come in." She took me to the dining room table, away from her kids and husband. "What is wrong?" she asked.

"Everything." I started to cry. She tried her best to console me until I was ready to talk. I told her about Tiffany. She didn't act surprised, or try to blame me.

"How long has this been going on?"

"Months. Eight? Nine?"

"Obviously, you want a change." I nodded. "It will start with breaking up with her."

"And then what?"

"And then you work on your marriage with Bellamy."

I shook my head. "I can't. I can't be with Bellamy anymore."

"Don't say that."

"How could I possibly be? I have wronged him. I have betrayed him. I can't bring myself to look at him and still feel alright with myself. This morning, he made me breakfast despite my absence in his life. I felt like killing myself."

She took a deep breath. "Do you think Bellamy still loves you?" I nodded. "Then why leave him? Have you stopped to consider how hurt he'd be if you left him? Do you know what that might do to him?"

I hadn't thought of how he'd feel if I left. I didn't have an answer.

"It's not too late, AJ. Don't give up on love. Don't leave a good man when you've already got him. You won't feel better afterwards. And I dare say, he won't either."

"I just can't face him."

"I know. Let's figure out how to go about this together," she said.

I was pleased to hear that. I didn't feel alone anymore. She said *we*.

The next evening, I went over to Tiffany's. The weight of the situation rested heavily on my shoulders. I wish I could avoid it. I knew I couldn't… if I wanted to enjoy my new found vigor with Bellamy.

"I want to move on from this relationship," I said to her after she let me in.

"I know," she said. I was shocked. She was calm… so calm it was troubling.

"You're alright with that?"

"What do you think?"

"I don't know."

"I'm crazy, I know," she said. "But that is usually within the confines of consent. Once it is withdrawn, I tend to do the right thing."

"I am sorry."

She chuckled. "You'll be fine." Then the tears streamed down from her eyes.

I left her then. I felt awful, but I was grateful to her. She made it easy for me. She didn't call or try to visit me anymore. I saw her in church a few times, and then I stopped seeing her. I didn't want to ask, but I was sure she had gone to Africa.

In this dark moment, another man came into my life. He reminded me of who I was, how much he cared about me, and that I was not forsaken. I mattered and he still had a plan for my life. If I would trust him, he would put all the broken pieces back together better than they were before. I wasn't the same person I was before. He saw my baggage and still loved me. I didn't have to be perfect. I didn't have to be a chameleon or perform. I prayed, and I knew he forgave me. Now I could receive this unconditional love that He had been trying to give me all this time. I took Him by the hand, and He helped me clean up *my* mess. Yes. This time it was the Lord. There wasn't this major hazmat crew just GOD, me, a few close friends, and a lot of elbow grease. We had to go through room by room and rebuild or clear out. Just like a physical house, my life had many rooms that needed to be brought into order from church to finances.

I was very good at setting up boundaries. This perimeter made me feel safe but at times it became my prison. I was locked away with my thoughts of feeling less of myself and longing to be wanted and accepted for me, not what I could do. One of the first things that I had to do was find my safe place. Where could I go and speak freely about what I was feeling and not be judged. Who would fight for me and with me? Who would provide wise counsel when I felt lost?

"It's not enough that you feel better about yourself," Dasha said to me. "You have to learn to live with Bellamy again."

"I believe that," I said.

"It's not the easiest thing. I suggest you meet a counselor."

I frowned. "Bellamy wouldn't agree to meet a counselor. He'd just say he was alright."

"He may not see the need to see one, but tell him he'll be doing this for the two of you. Let him know you believe your marriage will be better for it if you both saw one."

"Ok. Thank you. I will try."

Once I told Bellamy about seeing a counselor with me, he saw the need too. He didn't ask a lot of questions. In a week's time, we sat in front of a counselor, unburdening. I learned to unpack all the baggage of unrealistic expectations, unspoken expectation, fear, insecurity, hurt, abandonment, and rejection. I had to work on my individual issues before we could work on our marriage.

During our third meeting with the counselor, I told Bellamy I had a confession to make.

"What is it?" he said, turning to face me. It was obvious he hadn't been expecting it.

"I cheated," I said. He felt weak. I could see the energy sap from his face. "With Tiffany." I began to cry.

He passed me a handkerchief. He didn't let me proceed. He told me he understood, and that he was pleased I was finally coming clean about it. I was certain he thought Tiffany and I only shared kisses.

"I will never do that again, I promise," I said to him. "I will love you better."

We made incredible progress after that day. I found out I could live with him again and actually enjoy it.

By the time it was our last trip to the counselor's office, I believed I was a much better person. I began to think of Bellamy and I as a collective, not individuals. Two of the areas this reflected was in our finances and religion.

CHAPTER 8

Church had always been my thing. We both believed in God, but I was the more spiritual one. Bellamy would always say it was the way I was raised. For years I tried to convert him. Sounds so silly now in hindsight.

So where was the church during our storm? Around. Lack of trust, guilt and shame kept us from reaching out. I didn't want to be the subject of the next big scandal and could we really trust these people with our story? I had been let down so many times before…

At twenty-eight, I still felt so young and so naive. I was searching for something… someone to approve of me. No matter how many accolades I got, there were none that compared to a father. I longed to hear the words; *I am proud of you.* I had been married for two years, but still felt this way.

So, as I sat in the parking lot that hot July day, he ran to my car and said; I need you. I was stunned. I didn't think such a great man would say those words to me. I didn't believe I had anything to offer him. He was the pastor of a growing church.

He was renowned. People paid attention to his words and hung onto his advice like gold. For me, I was the person that was always overlooked.

He must have noticed the blank look on my face, so he said it again. My heart raced. I didn't know what to say. I smiled and said I would come visit the church some time.

I drove home with butterflies in my stomach. Those three words swirled around in my head. Maybe this was my purpose since I was no longer happy at our current church. I had gone to his church because a friend had been celebrating her anniversary, and had invited me. I had thought I'd just drop in unnoticed, and then fade out in the same vein. This was something new. A fresh start in a place we had never been before. I began to attend service at the church.

It started out great. I enjoyed services. I compelled Bellamy to join me. He was slow to oblige, but my energy was polarizing. He began to follow me there. The pastor talked a lot about his old life, and how he used to live a reckless life. He appreciated his new life now, and preached that anyone was capable of becoming new. Each day, I felt the burden of inadequacies I carried leave me. It was relieving.

It didn't last long before I began to feel a shift. More people began to attend. It was like there was a big campaign and people responded. But he was attracting people that were of his old life. I realized the pastor's demons had showed up and he was not resisting them. What about all the things he preached and all the people that he had helped to get delivered? What was really going on! It went from bad to worse very quickly.

Bellamy noticed the change and spoke with me a few times about it. Mentally, he checked out. His attendance was less and less and when he came he just sat there. I hung on, hoping. I was certain the pastor who had uplifted me so much in such short time, would come around. I waited—for the change or the release to leave. I kept hearing *stay*. I couldn't tell whose voice I was hearing. As a minister and intercessor in the church, I had to have a strong reason to leave.

I stayed. And then the news came. He was committing fornication with the young women in the church. I tried not to believe it, but I couldn't convince myself not to. I looked up to this man; he had become my spiritual father. He was supposed to watch over and protect his children. I didn't understand but I had to trust God.

Eventually, it got better. He said he was sorry and had taken the step to change. I believed him. I was foolish. I found out later that he was incapable of changing. My trust was broken once again. This man who saw my vulnerability; this man I thought would help me; was just a conman.

I would search and search until I understood that the church was not the apostle, prophet, teacher, evangelist, or teacher, but God. I could never put more trust in a man or woman than I put in God. They are vessels that He chooses to use. They were never meant to be put up on a pedestal and I did it for years.

Every time their voice carried more weight than God or my husband, I was left disappointed. He taught me not all counsel was wise and there was an order to this. Bellamy was the head of our household, not my pastor. I had to submit to my husband as unto the Lord.

Now, as I began to submit, he could love me the way he was supposed to… Not necessarily the way I wanted. Let's be honest, me and God don't always agree about how things should be done, but His plan is always the right one. I had to learn the balance of my need to help others and my duty as his wife. Bellamy and our home was and is my first ministry before I ever stepped on a stage.

The things I saw almost made me bitter, but it didn't succeed. It was our faith in God that rescued us from the brink of despair. You know that place called divorce. It allowed us to navigate the torrential waves and return safely home to each other the way it was meant to be from the beginning of time.

There was no scandal or condemnation, just a loving father welcoming us home. Then he placed us in a ministry where we could grow together with Him.

CHAPTER 9

Two and a half years after meeting Bellamy, it became clear we were going to walk down the aisle. By now, Dasha was already married and nursing her first child.

"Your finances, you and Bellamy's, have you had a discussion about that?" she asked me during one of my visits.

"Not yet."

"Why's that? It's pretty important."

"I know. But I am not bringing it up if he doesn't."

"I see," she said, putting her child on the bed. "At least, do you have an idea what you'd be doing with your finances once you're married to him?"

Finances was always one of the great debates I heard growing up. I saw men that controlled all the money and the woman had nothing; those that worked as a team, and those with a secret stash. I longed to be Bellamy's partner, but life had taught me never to let the right hand know what the left hand is doing. If he knows what you have, he can take it from you. He will leave you with nothing. I had vowed to never allow myself to get into that predicament. This was another bag that Bellamy didn't know about.

"I will definitely have separate accounts just in case it does not work out. I don't want to depend on him for anything. So, surely, we will keep everything separate."

"At least you know what you want," she said. "You only now need to be sure it is alright with him."

I didn't need to ask Dasha how she handled family finances with her husband. He was pretty comfortable, and didn't mind carrying the family. Dasha merely needed to make input.

"Some men are better at managing money and making budgets," Dasha said. "If this is Bellamy's strong area, you'll need to find out. You are not lousy with money, but you're not the best when keeping money is involved."

I laughed. Dasha had often said this. I didn't spend money because I was extravagant or insatiable, I spent money a lot out of my kindness for others.

For Bellamy and I, with the infertility appointments, trips with Tiffany and general bad spending, I began to feel the pressure. Bellamy was spending most of his extra money getting gigs and buying equipment.

As we began to rebuild, I had to have some very hard conversations about what I had been doing with the finances. It wasn't his debt and my debt, it was *our* debt. We had to find a system that worked best for our family. I didn't need another accountability partner. We balanced each other out. No, we didn't always agree, but we found out we had more together than we did a part. I had no idea what he was bringing to the table and vice versa. I had ignored Dasha's counsel.

As the head, he was built to carry the weight of our household. I was not. I was good with numbers but not the stress of carrying a household alone. Bellamy worked in an office in the day, and on his music at night. He was very talented, but it didn't pay the bills. I made more money than he did, thus the separation of funds. All those months of distance really took a toll, but now there was a sigh of relief. He wasn't the monster I had seen as a child or experienced from controlling boyfriends. He just wanted what was best for me... for us.

He didn't have a problem with me helping a friend or giving to the church, but he didn't like seeing me taken advantage of. I had a bleeding heart for every sad story. The wrong people could smell it a mile away like a shark smells blood in the water and attacks. I would give out of the kindness of my heart but their motives were not pure and I would find myself lying to Bellamy or burying my wet face in his chest from the disappointment. I would be over it in a few days but he would carry the pain and frustration for me for years to come.

As I listened to his heart, I knew I had judged him harshly. The control I blamed him for I was kind of walking in myself. I wasn't allowing him to be my husband in this area and I was determined to change that. We settled on a joint account for all the bills and then he would have his money to do with what he wanted and vice versa. I still needed that sense of independence. Something to call my own. The way his shoulders rose that day and his chest poked out was everything. There was a confidence that returned.

CHAPTER 10

I looked at my husband differently now, my ears were open to hear his words, and my heart longed for his love. I had my best friend back. The guy that made me smile. The guy that hugged me and I would get lost in his arms. The guy that supported me in all my endeavors. The guy that pushed me when I wanted to quit because he saw greatness in me. The guy that loved me like Christ loved the church. The guy that provided for his family with little thought for himself. The guy that once found comfort in my words. With a healed heart, I no longer saw his faults but all the qualities that I had loved from the beginning.

This was the turning point. I stopped feeling like I had to be perfect or defend myself. I wasn't sleeping with the enemy, but we did have to start facing our enemy head on. The enemy of division, discord, distraction, abandonment, rejection, perfection, unrealistic expectations, and comparison to name a few. We had dressed them up, but they were still lurking beneath the shadows setting traps and hiding their hands. We had become so accustomed to looking at each other and pointing fingers that we were missing all that had transpired in the spirit realm. We had to turn on the lights in some very dark areas.

How did we do that? First of all, prayer. We both had to have a little talk with Jesus. Do you remember that song growing up? We had to share our frustration and pain with someone that could handle it and wanted to see us succeed. He created us and ordained our union so who better to talk to than Abba? Before we ever started working on us we had to work on ourselves.

Then, we started talking. Simple conversations at first. How is the weather? What do you want to eat? Where do you see us in five years? We started out by reconnecting with each other on a basic level like you would when dating. From that point, we allowed the conversations to organically go to a deeper level. As we got back to that place-the foundation, it was easier to talk about the harder things without offense.

Sure, it took time for the healing to completely happen but at least now we were on the right track and God was at the center of it all. The same forgiveness that God gives to us *daily* we had to dig deep and give it to each other and focus on the future *daily*. Forgiveness is not a one and done but a decision you make every day until your heart and mind can align and the sting from the pain dissipates like water on hot asphalt.

I stood before my family and vowed to love honor and cherish Bellamy until death do us part. Sometimes I thought that was literally what was going to happen. I wanted happily ever after so bad, but it sometimes felt like a nightmare. I quickly learned that marriage was made up of intentional actions and happily ever after was built not given. It was forged with the hammer of communication, caulked with truth, and secured by the scaffolding of accountability, and painted by faith. I was no longer just a woman with a ring or many words but nothing of substance to say. I was now a wise wife ready to build.

Everyone needs a little help along the way. Here are a few resources you can find at www.thecassandrawilliams.com to help you on your journey of redemption and becoming a wise wife that knows how to build:

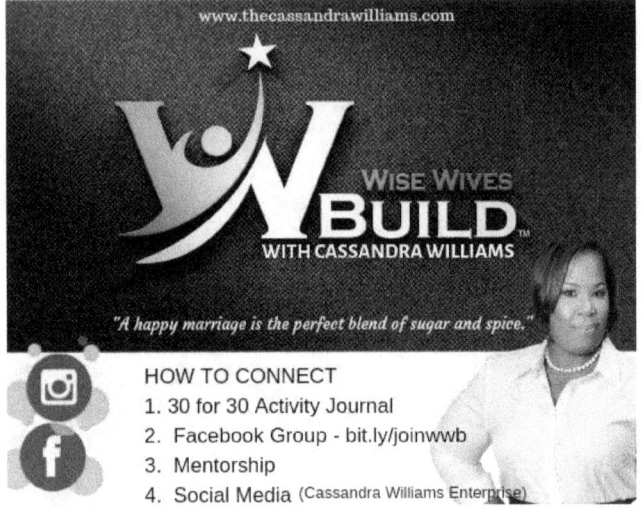

ABOUT THE AUTHOR

Casandra Williams is a wife of 20 plus years, mother, author, speaker, Certified Professional Life and Empowerment Coach and founder of Wise Wives Build.

I Believe...

- An expert or authority is not always the person with plaques and degrees covering the walls, but the one that has paid the price of living through the blood, sweat and tears to carry the message.
- The human spirit, much like water, is very resilient. Although it runs into obstacles, it chips away at them to become something beautiful.
- We are all imperfectly perfect. Your past does not have to determine your future.
- Everyone has an inner genius that is waiting to be released, but you have to do the work.
- A ring does not make you a wise wife. You could just be a girl with a ring.

What I Do…

- Empower people, especially women, to let go of old mentality and live in victory by dealing with the past, embracing where you are now, and moving forward.
- Equip women to repair the breaches (holes) in their life to break cycles.
- Encourage people to see things from all perspectives so they can effective resolve conflicts.
- Train wives to use practical tools and techniques to build healthy husbands, children, business, ministries, and lives for themselves.

Signature Speaking Topics…

- **Where's Daddy?** - This talk helps women deal with the emotions they have carried around for years because they longed for the love of their father. Whether he was just absent, incarcerated, or died unexpectedly the feelings of anger, rejection, abandonment, and sadness are the same.
- **Proverbs 31 Woman** - Who said you can't have it all? This lesson uses Proverbs 31 as the backdrop for the Godly character we need as businesswomen and Wise Wives that are ready to build healthy families.
- **The Power of Forgiveness** - Women are carriers by nature. Our bodies can carry a baby for 9 months and

then we carry them in our hearts. Unless we learn how to release, we carry hurt, pain and disappointment in the same way. During this discussion we explore different ways process through forgiving yourself, others, and God.

- **Goal Setting & Vision Board Creation** - This workshop helps you take all the ideas swirling around in your head and place them on paper. Those ideas are then turned into smart goals and a vision board that will keep you focused and motivated.

- **Overcoming Identity Theft** - Sometimes you can lose yourself in the midst of life's challenges or helping others. This lecture helps you put safeguards in place to ensure that you are not taken advantage or giving away your birthright ever again. People will continue to do whatever you allow.

- **A Victor's Heart** - This one is for the fighters. You may not be the strongest or the fastest, but you have the tenacity of the bulldog. Once you set your eyes on a goal you will not stop until you see it to completion. Whether something happened to you, you made a bad choice, or you were led on a journey, you can come out victorious.